KU-181-300

Franklin Watts
First published in Great Britain in 2020
by The Watts Publishing Group

Text © Steve Barlow and Steve Skidmore 2020
Illustrations © The Watts Publishing Group 2020
Cover design: Cathryn Gilbert and Peter Scoulding

ISBN 978 1 4451 6976 7
ebook ISBN 978 1 4451 6974 3
Library ebook ISBN 978 1 4451 6975 0

1 3 5 7 9 10 8 6 4 2

Printed in Great Britain

MIX
Paper from
responsible sources
FSC
www.fsc.org FSC® C104740

Franklin Watts
An imprint of
Hachette Children's Group
Part of The Watts Publishing Group
Carmelite House
50 Victoria Embankment
London EC4Y 0DZ

An Hachette UK Company
www.hachette.co.uk

www.hachettechildrens.co.uk

Mission Statement

You are the hero of this mission.

Each section of this book is numbered. At the end of most sections, you will have to make a choice. The choice you make will take you to a different section of the book.

Some of your choices will help you to complete the adventure successfully. But if you make the wrong choice, death may be the best you can hope for! Because even dying is better than being UNDEAD and becoming a slave of the monsters you have sworn to destroy!

Dare you go up against a world of monsters?

All right, then.

Let's see what you've got...

Introduction

You are an agent of **G.H.O.S.T.** — Global Headquarters Opposing Supernatural Threats.

Our world is under constant attack from supernatural horrors that lurk in the shadows. It's your job to make sure they stay there.

You have studied all kinds of monsters, and know their habits and behaviour. You are an expert in disguise, able to move among monsters in human form as a spy. You are expert in all forms of martial arts. G.H.O.S.T. has supplied you with weapons, equipment and other assets that make you capable of destroying any supernatural creature.

G.H.O.S.T.

You are based at Arcane Hall, a spooky and secret-laden mansion. Your butler, Cranberry, is another G.H.O.S.T. agent who assists you in all your adventures, providing you with information and backup.

Your life at Arcane Hall is comfortable and peaceful; but you know that at any moment, the G.H.O.S.T. High Command can order you into action in any part of the world...

Go to 1.

1

You are at a stadium in London, watching your favourite football team and cheering them on.

Your phone rings with the *Ghostbusters* theme. You answer it. "Not now, Cranberry! We're playing against United and they've just scored!"

"Very disappointing, I'm sure," says Cranberry, "but you're needed at the British Museum."

To tell Cranberry you'll go at the end of the match, go to 12.

To leave the stadium at once, go to 31.

You fire a Keep Mum round at one mummy. While it struggles helplessly in the net, you have time to reload and take out the second mummy before it can grab you.

"Well done, Agent," says Cranberry. "That appears to be all the escaped mummies accounted for. And I have some interesting news about Selma Masry."

"The Curator of Egyptology at the British Museum?"

"Exactly. She's been spotted at Heathrow airport."

"That's impossible," you say. "I saw Curator Masry being kidnapped by a bunch of mummies — if she's at Heathrow, how did she get away, and where did the mummies go?"

"Well, Border Control say she's just boarded a flight to Cairo."

"Cairo, Egypt?"

"Well done, agent!"

"There are a lot of mummies in Egypt," you say thoughtfully.

To follow Curator Masry, go to 15.

To dismiss the sighting as the wrong person, go to 30.

3

As you creep along an avenue of ram-headed sphinxes, you hear chanting from the inner court of the temple: "Amun-re! Amun-re!"

The Mummies' Institute is getting started, you think.

You use the drone to spy out ways of getting to the precinct unseen. There seem to be two possibilities. You make your choice.

To head there via the Hypostyle Court, go to 38.

To approach via the Sacred Lake, go to 46.

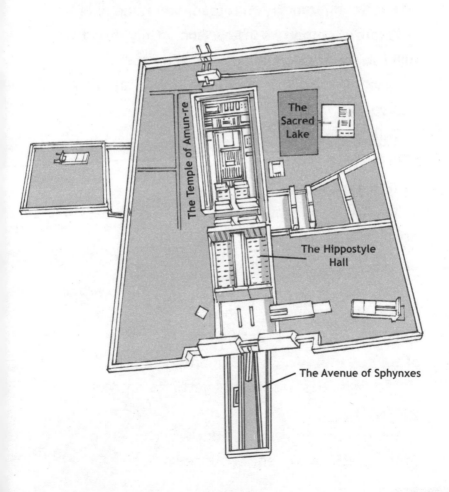

4

You raise the Keep Mum launcher and fire.

A weighted net shoots out and wraps itself around the nearest mummy, who is instantly so tangled up that it can't move.

But as you struggle to reload, you remember (too late) Cranberry's instruction: "Only effective against one or two mummies at a time..."

Reloading takes time you don't have and now you're surrounded by angry mummies.

Go to 33.

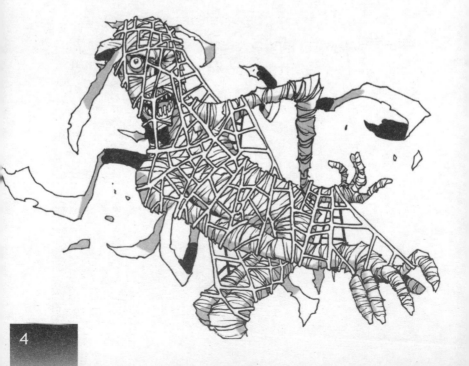

You check the dial of your YMWLI weapon is still set to 1,500 years, and fire.

The mummies in the precinct collapse into dust. Some try to stop you, but you are out of their reach, and the few that try to climb towards you lose their grip and fall. The flying stones that were coming together to rebuild the temple crash to the ground.

In the midst of the chaos, you see Curator Masry waving her arms as she chants a spell — and disappears.

You abseil down from your perch and run to where she was standing. The Book of the Dead is still where she left it. You send an image of the open page to Cranberry for translation.

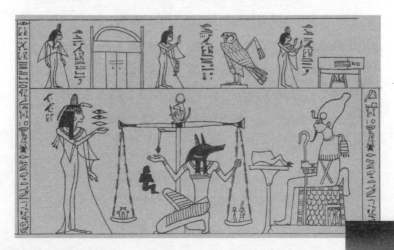

Tense moments pass before Cranberry says, "Not good, Agent. Just before she disappeared, Curator Masry cast a spell to take her to the Land of the Dead."

To declare your mission completed, go to 28.

To follow Masry to the Land of the Dead, go to 35.

6

"Mummies can't just come alive," you tell the Curator.

"Of course not," she says angrily. "But a mummy is the mortal remains of a pharaoh, a queen or an important priest or official: legend says they can be reanimated if their ka — their soul — is brought back from the afterlife by a spell read from the ancient Book of the Dead. And mummies are very, very strong."

"Maybe," you say, "but they're covered in bandages, and dry as dust. And if they're dry, they'll burn."

To go into the museum alone, go to 44.

To take Curator Masry with you, go to 22.

7

"I'll figure it out as I go," you tell Yussuf.

Ignoring his protests, you blow the museum door open with a small explosive charge and burst in.

You make your way to the main exhibition hall. Here, among statues of ancient Egyptian gods and pharaohs, and cases of archaeological finds, you come upon a gathering of lurching mummies.

As they turn towards you, growling, you aim the YMWLI weapon at them. *Let's see how powerful this is*, you think. You pull the trigger.

Nothing happens.

Uh-oh.

Then the mummies are upon you.

Go to 33.

8

You hold Masry while Osiris takes your heart from the scales and replaces it with hers. The scales move instantly. Masry's heart is much heavier than the feather.

Anubis signals for you to release Masry. You do so and step back.

Masry turns to run, but too late. A ghastly creature with a lion's mane and crocodile's head rises from the pit and snatches her in its jaws before sinking back into the darkness. Curator Masry sought power in the Afterlife. Instead, she has found only everlasting oblivion.

Anubis gestures again...

Go to 50.

You step out of hiding, firing your Keep Mum. As one mummy struggles in its net, you drop the launcher and fire your WHAM gun with your right hand and YMWLI with your left.

Either side of you, mummies grind to a halt as the WHAM's WHack A Mummy spray dries on their bandages or they crumble into dust in the beam of the YMWLI.

You whistle in appreciation of the new weapon's power. "Your Mummy *really* Wouldn't Like It!"

Before long, the room is clear of reanimated mummies — but Curator Masry is nowhere to be seen. You race outside just in time to see a helicopter taking off from the museum forecourt.

Cursing, you head back to the Spook Truck where Yussuf is waiting. "I've stopped the mummies here," you tell him, "but Masry is the

one who is reanimating them. She could have gone to find more."

"Then I think I know where she will go," says Yussuf.

To listen to Yussuf's suggestion, go to 49.
To ignore it, go to 27.

10

You race from the museum to the Spook Truck. You'll need more weapons to deal with a mass outbreak of mummies!

"Take the WHAM gun," advises Cranberry over the comms link.

You check labels. "WHack A Mummy gun — check. And I'll take the Keep Mum too."

"Effective," Cranberry comments, "but only against one or two mummies at a time. Wait — news coming in. Mummies are attacking the Lord Mayor's Show. The show is a big street parade with floats, dancers and marching bands — you don't want it wrecked by mummy mayhem."

"Okay, I'm on it."

To take the Spook Truck, go to 32.
To go on foot, go to 25.

11

You use all your martial arts skills against the mummies — but being undead, they feel no pain: and they are VERY strong.

They grab you by the wrists and ankles. For a moment they swing you to and fro... Then they tear you in half. It really hurts.

Pull yourself together and go back to 1.

12

"Everything in the museum has been there for centuries," you tell Cranberry. "Whatever's wrong can wait until the end of the match."

Cranberry sniffs. "If you say so, Agent."

Ten minutes later United are two up and your phone rings again. This time it's the Director General of G.H.O.S.T. and she is not happy!

"When I say, 'Jump!', you jump, Agent! Right away! Am I clear?"

You're on a yellow card already. Annoying the DG any more is a sure way to get to red.

"Yes, ma'am," you mutter. "I'm on my way."

Go to 31.

13

You doze fitfully as the Spook Truck races towards Luxor.

Yussuf wakes you. "According to the radio, there's a big thunderstorm over the Valley of the Kings."

"I didn't think it rained there."

"It doesn't," says Yussuf grimly.

Cranberry calls. "An army of mummies from the Valley of the Kings is descending on the Temple of Karnak."

You sigh. "This just gets better and better."

"Something very big is happening." Yussuf looks frightened. "I think Curator Masry is trying to raise the power of Amun — the greatest of the Egyptian gods. If she can control that then Masry will be all-powerful — the world will be doomed."

You call up a map of Karnak from the internet and upload it to your helmet visor's head-up display. As soon as the Spook Truck arrives at the temple, you take your weapons and make your way inside.

You check the display. The Precinct of Amun is the oldest part of the temple. You take a fist-sized drone from your backpack and send it into the temple. Sure enough, its camera reveals a huge gathering of mummies in the precinct. In the centre, wearing the mask of Anubis, stands a woman you recognise from her clothing as Curator Masry.

This doesn't look good.

To try to reach Masry without being seen, go to 3.

To launch an immediate attack, go to 39.

14

You decide to stay in the truck, hoping the traffic will clear. But it doesn't, and before long your phone rings. It's the Director General of G.H.O.S.T.

"You're too late," she yells. "While you've been sitting there like a spare part, the mummies have taken over London! You're fired..."

Go to 1.

15

Two hours later you are in the Phantom Flyer, heading for Cairo.

You call Cranberry on the comms link. "I need more information. How does the whole reanimation thing work? Curator Masry said the mummies' souls had to be brought back from the afterlife."

"That's right," says Cranberry, "using a spell from the ancient Egyptian Book of the Dead."

You shiver. "Sounds creepy."

"You're a G.H.O.S.T. agent," Cranberry reminds you. "'Creepy' is what you do."

The Phantom Flyer is faster than the Curator's commercial flight, and you are waiting in the arrivals hall by the time she leaves the airport. You tail her to the Egyptian Museum.

To confront the Curator, go to 40.
To keep watch and call for backup, go to 34.

16

Angrily, you hurl Masry from you. She disappears into the pit with a scream.

But the scales of judgment move again: your heart is now heavier than the feather. You have shown anger, and have failed Anubis's test.

With a gesture, Anubis banishes you to the pit of lost souls; you follow your enemy into oblivion.

Temper, temper! Go back to 1.

17

You grab a spear from the wall rack — but it is very old. The shaft crumbles to dust in your hands and the steel spearhead clatters on to the floor.

Before you can react, you are surrounded by mummies.

Go to 33.

18

You make your demand at the top of your voice.

Anubis is angry. He raises his staff. You find yourself flying through the air and tumbling into the pit.

Instinctively, you know that you are being banished to the underworld where those who have offended the gods simply cease to exist. There is no way back.

Don't mess with the gods, 'cos the gods don't mess. Go back to 1.

19

You glance at the Egyptian museum door that the Curator used. "There's no time to lose. I'll go in this way."

You blast the door open and go inside, along a dark corridor. You have hardly taken six paces before you are clubbed on the head from behind. You slump to the floor, unconscious.

When you come to, it takes you a few seconds to realise that you have been disarmed — and you are in some kind of stone box. A grinding noise makes you look up — and give a cry of fear.

You are in a sarcophagus — a stone coffin — and mummies are closing the lid on you. They seem to enjoy doing to you what was once done to all of them. The difference is, they were dead at the time.

You scream and scream, but no one hears. You are helpless — and so is Cairo.

You've been put back in the box. Go back to 1.

20

You raise the WHAM gun and fire.

A powerful spray shoots from the barrel of the gun. The spray contains a fast-setting glue that penetrates the mummies' bandages and makes them hard. Gradually, all the mummies grind to a halt.

You pat the empty gun. "That's the way to WHack A Mummy."

"I'll have the police tidy up here," says Cranberry. "And I'll try and find out where the mummies took Director Masry. I don't think this is over yet."

If you've already dealt with the mummies at Cleopatra's Needle, go to 41.

If you haven't, go to 48.

21

You stride forward and snatch the phone. "No, no," you tell the bemused mummies. "You'll never get all of you in the shot that way. I'll do it..." You point the camera and shake your head. "Now, you're in, but I can't get the Needle — tell you what, climb on the wall — yes, behind

you — up you go! Up, up!" The mummies climb
hesitantly on to the wall between the pavement
and the River Thames. "That's better — I
still can't get you all in though — take a step
backwards..."

SPLASH! You look over the wall. The mummies
have fallen in the river. Their bandaged bodies
are already starting to come apart as they float
away, you wave them goodbye.

"Rest in pieces..."

**If you haven't dealt with the mummies at
the Lord Mayor's Show, go to 37.**

If you have, go to 41.

You creep through dark exhibition halls until you reach the Ancient Egypt section. Curator Masry flicks a switch and lights come on to reveal the hall is full of lurching mummies! One reaches for you, but sees the flame pistol and stops.

"What's the matter?" you ask. "Do you want to live forever?" Of course you do, you think, that's why you're a mummy.

The mummy reaches out again. You fire, engulfing it in flames. The other mummies lurch away — except for a couple, who grab Curator Masry and carry her off. "Help me!" she cries.

Cranberry's voice sounds from your comms link. "Agent, the police report that mummies are starting to leave the museum — you must stop them!"

To help Curator Masry, go to 47.
To stop the escaping mummies, go to 10.

23

You find the delivery entrance unguarded and sneak in.

In the museum's main exhibition hall, you find a gathering of lurching mummies, and others that are still lifeless. A woman you recognise as Curator Masry stands over an inert mummy. As you watch, she puts on the gold mask of a High Priestess of Anubis, jackal-headed god of the Land of the Dead. She opens a large book and begins to read.

"Cranberry, I've found Curator Masry," you breathe into your comms link. "I think she's about to reanimate more mummies."

To break up the ceremony, go to 9.
To wait and see what happens, go to 43.

You use the drone's controls to bring it swooping through the pillars of the Hypostyle Court. The cats immediately start to chase it, leaping into the air and batting at it with their bandaged paws.

While they're busy, you leave the hall. With the aid of a grapnel hook and climbing rope, you scale the pylon guarding the gateway to the precinct, where Curator Masry and the mummies are still chanting.

You reach the top of the pylon. Even if the mummies spot you up here, it will take them time to follow — and you can see everything that is going on in the precinct below.

As you watch, Masry spreads her arms wide. The earth begins to rumble and shake beneath your feet. To your astonishment, stones begin to move. The ruined Temple of Amun is rebuilding itself before your eyes!

To attack the mummies with the YMWLI, go to 5.

To attack with the WHAM, go to 42.

25

You head for the parade, but as you shoulder your way through the crowds, Cranberry's voice sounds in your ear. "I now have a report that mummies have been spotted on the Thames embankment, at Cleopatra's Needle."

"Give me a break, Cranberry," you complain. "I can't be in two places at once!"

To head for the Lord Mayor's Show, go to 37.

To head for Cleopatra's Needle, go to 48.

26

You bow to Anubis. "Lord of the dead, this woman has done evil. I have come to take her away, if that is your will."

Curator Masry points at you. "Do not listen to this unbeliever! I am the true servant of the gods..."

A great voice — the voice of Anubis — echoes inside your head. "ARE YOU WILLING TO BE JUDGED?"

You hesitate. Anubis is the god of death. Here in the Land of the Dead, his word is law.

To accept Anubis's judgment, go to 36.

To demand that Anubis judges only Curator Masry, go to 18.

27

"I've no time to listen to guesses," you tell Yussuf as you climb into the Spook Truck and speed away.

Heading back to your Phantom Flyer, you call Cranberry. "Track that helicopter. I want to know where she's going."

Cranberry reports that the helicopter is heading south along the River Nile. "Right," you say, "I'll follow it in the Phantom Flyer."

But when you get to the airport, you find that it is closed because of a sandstorm. Even in the few steps from the car park to the terminal, you are almost blinded by flying sand. No flights are taking off or landing. You are stranded.

You try to get some sleep as you wait for the storm to clear. You have already fouled up by not listening to Yussuf, so you have left yourself nowhere to go. Then your phone buzzes. It is the Director General of G.H.O.S.T.

"The city of Luxor is alive with mummies," she snaps, "which is more than I can say for you, Agent — you're toast!"

Go back to 1.

28

You sigh with relief. "Well, that's the end of her, and good riddance."

Yussuf's voice crackles from your helmet-radio. "I wouldn't be too sure about that..."

"Nonsense!" you snap. "I'm off to a nice hotel and a soft bed..."

You break off and look around in horror as the earth moves again. Great shadowy shapes are rising out of the ground.

You realise that Masry has awoken the gods of ancient Egypt — cat-headed Bastet; scarab beetle Khepri; Anubis, god of the underworld; falcon-headed Horus; ibis-headed Thoth; and many other strange beings. Thunderclouds swirl in the tortured sky and lightning flashes around them.

Cranberry's voice sounds faintly from your comms link. "Well, that's about it for this planet..."

You always thought the Egyptian gods were kind of cool. That was when they were thousands of miles away and thousands of years in the past.

Go back to 1.

29

You fire your flame pistol.

But you are surrounded by dry, dusty exhibits. They catch fire quickly. Soon, there is no way out.

As the mummies burst into flames, you realise that you and Curator Masry will share their fate!

Your chances of stopping the mummies just went up in smoke! Go back to 1.

30

You shake your head. "The Border Agency must have the wrong person. I'm not shooting off to Cairo on a wild goose chase."

You head back to Arcane Manor for a night's rest.

However, it is still dark when you get a phone call from the furious Director General of G.H.O.S.T.

"Cairo is swarming with live mummies," she yells, "while you're lazing in bed. You're fired!"

Sleeping on the job, eh? That rates a big tut tut. In fact a King Tut. Go back to 1.

You drive to the museum in your Spook Truck, checking your video and audio comms links that allow Cranberry, back at Arcane Manor, to see and hear everything you do.

"Do you read me, Cranberry?"

"Loud and clear, Agent."

You arrive at the museum to find the police have already sealed off the building.

The officer in charge steps forward. "Stay back! We've been told there are mummies on the loose in there!"

You show him your ID. "What mummies?"

The officer points to a young woman. "This is the Curator of Egyptology at the museum. Ask her."

The Curator nods. "My name is Selma Masry, and the officer is right. Our mummies are coming alive!"

To go straight into the museum, go to 44.
To find out more from the Curator, go to 6.

32

You set off in the Spook Truck, but some roads are closed for the Lord Mayor's Show and others are gridlocked. You are soon stuck in heavy traffic, going nowhere.

To stay with the truck, go to 14.
To abandon the truck, go to 25.

33

You remind yourself what you know about mummies. They're very, very strong, you recall as they reach out and grab you.

After a few seconds of agony, you can't think anything any more.

Go back to 1.

34

"This is a big museum," you tell Cranberry. "I'll need local help."

"Coming up," says Cranberry.

Half an hour later, a Spook Truck arrives with a young Egyptian at the wheel.

"I am Yussuf," he says cheerfully, "local agent of G.H.O.S.T. here in Cairo. What do you need?"

In the back of the truck you find a fully-charged flame pistol, WHAM gun and Keep Mum.

"There's this, too." Yussuf passes you an

odd-looking device. "It's new. We call it 'Your Mummy Wouldn't Like It' — YMWLI for short. Very powerful, but be careful — it's experimental, and tricky to operate."

To take the weapons and burst into the museum, go to 7.

To ask Yussuf for more information, go to 45.

"I have to follow her," you say. "She's reanimated mummies — who knows what else she may bring back to life?"

"If you're sure," says Cranberry unhappily. "Repeat after me..."

He reads out the spell. You repeat it and...

The world around you grows dim; you are in a land of darkness and shadows. Even the ground beneath your feet seems airy and unreal. You realise that you are present in the Land of the Dead only in spirit form; your body has remained behind in the living world.

You are in a great hall like the Hypostyle Court. The ghostly figure of Curator Masry stands beside you. Before you, the mighty jackal-headed Anubis sits on a huge golden throne. And this guy isn't a statue. At his feet gapes a great bottomless pit of eternal darkness.

To speak respectfully to Anubis, go to 26.

To demand that Anubis sends you and Masry back to the living world, go to 18.

"Judge us both!" you tell Anubis. "Then you will know where the truth lies!" Masry looks frightened.

A movement makes you look up. Above the hall hovers a gigantic goddess with the wings of a vulture. Anubis plucks a single feather from her and places it on one side of a set of scales.

The falcon-headed god Osiris steps from the shadows. He reaches out and plucks your heart from your chest, placing it in the other pan.

The scales waver — then the one holding the feather dips. Your heart is lighter than the feather; you have passed the test.

With a scream of rage, Masry throws herself at you. You grapple on the edge of the pit. Being stronger and better trained, you soon gain the upper hand.

To throw Masry into the pit, go to 16.
To call on Anubis to judge her, go to 8.

37

As you get close to the Lord Mayor's Show, you can hear the commentary over loudspeakers...

"...and coming along now, we have the Band of the Dragoon Guards playing a selection of musical hits... and next, a float sponsored by London Zoo with lots of cute pandas.

"Then, in their colourful robes and chains of office, we have the members of the Worshipful Guild of Fish-gutters... Here comes a steel band...

*and after them, an army of lurching mummies…
they've certainly gone to town on their outfits —
scary stuff!"*

You burst through the crowd and find yourself
face-to-bandages with the mummies.

To use your Keep Mum, go to 4.
To use your WHAM gun, go to 20.

38

As you make your way between the towering
columns of the Hypostyle Court, you hear
stealthy noises coming from all around you.

Suddenly, you are surrounded by glowing eyes.

You remember that ancient Egyptians made cat-mummies in honour of the goddess Bastet. These cats don't look like the sort that sit on your lap and purr. They look like the sort of cats that hiss and spit and try to claw your face off.

To back away and try the Sacred Lake instead, go to 46.

To try to distract the cat-mummies, go to 24.

39

You burst into the Precinct of Amun, firing with every weapon you have, using the tactics that served you well in the Egyptian Museum.

But this time, the mummies are ready for you, and there are hundreds of them.

Many fall; but as soon as you are out of ammunition, the remaining mummies close in.

Go to 11.

40

You stay out of sight as the Curator takes out a key and opens a side door of the museum. Once she is inside, you open the door with your

G.H.O.S.T. UE (Unauthorised Entry) kit and slip inside.

You sneak along a corridor. Hearing footsteps coming towards you, you duck into a side-room and close the door.

Unfortunately, the room turns out to be full of mummies — reanimated ones. They do not seem pleased to see you, and the door has locked itself behind you.

Oops.

Go to 33.

41

"You have a new target, Agent," says Cranberry. "I have reports that mummies are outside Buckingham Palace, gate-crashing the Changing of the Guard."

"A mummy's work is never done," you mutter as you head for the palace, "and neither is mine..."

As you get closer to the palace, you are almost trampled upon by fleeing tourists and guardsmen.

Outside the palace, two mummies are 'on guard', wearing bearskins and all. One carries his rifle upside down.

You raise your WHAM gun and pull the trigger. Nothing happens — you are out of WHAM spray.

To use the Keep Mum, go to 2.

To fight the mummies hand-to-hand, go to 11.

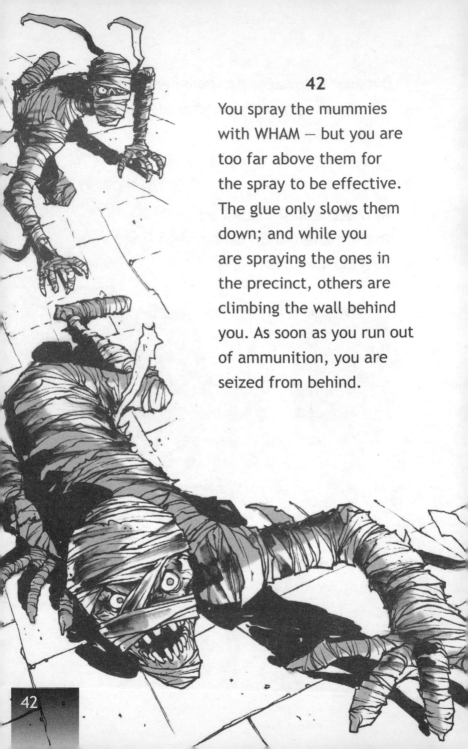

42

You spray the mummies with WHAM — but you are too far above them for the spray to be effective. The glue only slows them down; and while you are spraying the ones in the precinct, others are climbing the wall behind you. As soon as you run out of ammunition, you are seized from behind.

From far below, Curator Masry gives you a gloating look. "No afterlife for you!" she cackles. The mummies close in.

Go to 11.

43

You watch and wait.

Unfortunately, you are so intent on what Curator Masry is doing that you don't notice the stealthy footsteps and the rustle of bandages as mummies creep up behind you.

You are grabbed by many undead hands.

You can think of lots of really deadly martial arts moves you could use to defend yourself. Unfortunately, these all depend on having your arms and legs free and not held in the unbreakable grip of a bunch of mummies. Despite your struggles, they drag you before the Anubis-headed Curator Masry, who takes off her mask.

"Ah, there you are, mummy's boy!" she scoffs.

"I'm no mummy's boy," you protest.

"You are now!" She gestures to the mummies. "Nighty night."

Go to 33.

You check your flame pistol. "This will sort them out. Those mummies will wish they'd never been — er — mummified."

There are no lights in the museum. You creep silently through the exhibition halls until you reach the Ancient Egypt section.

It is very dark in here. You hear shuffling. You light your torch — and find yourself surrounded by mummies.

Go to 33.

You raise the YMWLI. "So how does it work?"

"A mummy isn't just bandages," Yussuf explains. "There's a body inside. The YMWLI makes the body age at the rate it would have done if it hadn't been mummified." He points. "There's a dial marked in years — the device won't work until you've set it."

"How many years?" you ask.

"Depends on how old the mummies are. We reckon 1,500 years is generally enough."

You set the dial to 1,500 years. "Okay," you say. "Now, what's my best way in?"

"There's a delivery entrance," says Yussuf. "Shall I show you?"

To ignore Yussuf's advice, go to 19.
To let Yussuf show you the way, go to 23.

The Sacred Lake is surrounded by what look like logs, but there are no mummies in sight. You start to wade through the stagnant water, holding your weapons above your head to keep them dry.

Too late, you realise that the 'logs' are moving. Then you remember that the ancient Egyptians mummified animals as well as people — animals like crocodiles...

The giant reptiles might be mummies, but there is nothing wrong with their teeth...

Go back to 1.

47

You follow the mummies and their struggling captive into an exhibition of Da Vinci drawings. You raise your flame pistol.

"Don't fire that in here!" screeches Cranberry in your earpiece. "Those drawings are priceless!"

"Okay, okay!"

You follow the mummies through some fire doors, down a flight of stairs and into a basement. The walls are lined with old-fashioned weapons — swords, spears and axes.

To use your flame pistol, go to 29.
To grab one of the weapons, go to 17.

48

Cleopatra's Needle is an obelisk, brought from Egypt to London two hundred years ago. Terrified tourists are running away from the dozen or so mummies lurching towards it. One tourist drops his phone. A mummy scoops it up, beckons the others to join it in front of the monument, and holds the phone at arm's length.

Cranberry, watching the scene through your head-cam, is puzzled. "What are they doing?"

You shake your head in disbelief. "They're taking selfies."

To use your Keep Mum on the mummies, go to 4.

To offer to take their picture, go to 21.

"Go on," you tell Yussuf.

"She will head for Luxor — for the temples of Luxor and Karnak, and the Valley of the Kings. There are many mummies there."

"Okay," you say. "Let's get to the airport."

You are halfway to Cairo International Airport when Cranberry calls. "Bad news, Agent. The airport has been closed by a sandstorm."

You groan. "How far is Luxor by road?"

"Eight hours," says Yussuf. "Get some rest. I'll drive."

Go to 13.

50

You awake to find yourself lying on the pavement of the Karnak Temple. The sun has just risen.

Yussuf stands over you. He gives a sigh of relief as he realises you're alive, and helps you to your feet.

"You're back!" Cranberry's voice is loud in your earpiece. "What happened?"

You shake your head. "I don't know how to explain it so you won't think I'm crazy. And if I do tell you, you've both got to promise never to tell anyone else, or they'll think we're *all* crazy..."

"All right," says Yussuf.

"Agreed," says Cranberry. "Mummy's the word."

EQUIPMENT

Phantom Flyer: For fast international and intercontinental travel, you use the Phantom Flyer, a supersonic business jet crammed full of detection and communication equipment and weaponry.

Spook Trucks: For more local travel you use one of G.H.O.S.T.'s fleet of Spook Trucks — heavily armed and armoured SUVs you requisition from local agents.

Flame Pistol — mummies don't like fire!

Keep Mum — a net is fired which surrounds and incapacitates a mummy

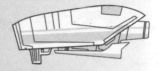

WHAM (WHack A Mummy) — sprays fast-hardening glue that solidifies mummy wrappings and renders them immobile

YMWLI (Your Mummy Wouldn't Like It) — mummy ageing device

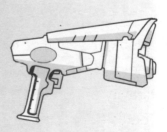

MONSTER HUNTER

I HERO

DEMON

STEVE BARLOW ⬦ STEVE SKIDMORE
Illustrated by PAUL DAVIDSON

EDGE

1

You are in India on a well-earned break from
saving the world (again).

You're visiting the world-famous Taj Mahal, built at the command of the emperor Shah Jahan in the 17th century to house the tomb of his wife.

Wandering around the gardens that surround the marble building, you observe a troop of macaque monkeys in the trees.

A local tour guide sees you admiring the creatures. "The monkeys look lovely, but my advice is to stay clear of them, they can be vicious!"

You think about all the supernatural creatures you have had to face in your career. "Thanks for the warning," you laugh. "But they're only monkeys!"

As you walk towards the tree, the monkeys drop down from the branches and head towards you. You are shocked to see them transforming! Their eyes burn red and their teeth grow into huge, razor-sharp fangs. You realise what they are. They aren't 'only monkeys'; they are demon monkeys ...

Continue the adventure in:
MONSTER HUNTER
DEMON

About the 2Steves

"The 2Steves" are one
of Britain's most popular
writing double acts for
young people, specialising
in comedy and adventure.

Together they have written many books, including the
I HERO Immortals series.

Find out what they've been up to at:
www.the2steves.net

About the illustrator:
Paul Davidson

Paul Davidson is a British
illustrator and comic book artist.

Have you completed these I HERO adventures?

I HERO Immortals — more to enjoy!

Dinosaur Hunter

978 1 4451 6963 7 pb
978 1 4451 6964 4 ebook

Fairy

978 1 4451 6969 9 pb
978 1 4451 6971 2 ebook

Knight

978 1 4451 6957 6 pb
978 1 4451 6959 0 ebook

Pirate Queen

978 1 4451 6954 5 pb
978 1 4451 6955 2 ebook

Samurai

978 1 4451 6960 6 pb
978 1 4451 6962 0 ebook

Witch

978 1 4451 6966 8 pb
978 1 4451 6967 5 ebook

Defeat all the baddies in Toons:

Killer Custard

978 1 4451 5930 0 pb
978 1 4451 5931 7 ebook

Robin Hamster

978 1 4451 5921 8 pb
978 1 4451 5922 5 ebook

Enter the Penguin

978 1 4451 5924 9 pb
978 1 4451 5925 6 ebook

Kung Fu Kitten

978 1 4451 5918 8 pb
978 1 4451 5919 5 ebook

Also by the 2Steves...

978 1 4451 5985 0

Tip can't believe his luck when he mysteriously wins tickets to see his favourite team in the cup final. But there's a surprise in store ...

978 1 4451 5892 1

Big baddie Mr Butt Hedd is in hot pursuit of the space cadets and has tracked them down for Lord Evil. But can Jet, Tip and Boo Hoo find a way to escape in a cunning disguise?

978 1 4451 5988 1

Jet and Tip get a new command from Master Control to intercept some precious cargo. It's time to become space pirates!

978 1 4451 5979 9

The goodies intercept a distress signal and race to the rescue. Then some eight-legged fiends appear ... Tip and Jet realise it's a trap!